What is the tortoise eating?

Can you jump like a kangaroo?

Beetle

Kangaroo

Sun

Meerkat

Can you spot the tarantula?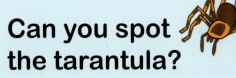

In the woodland

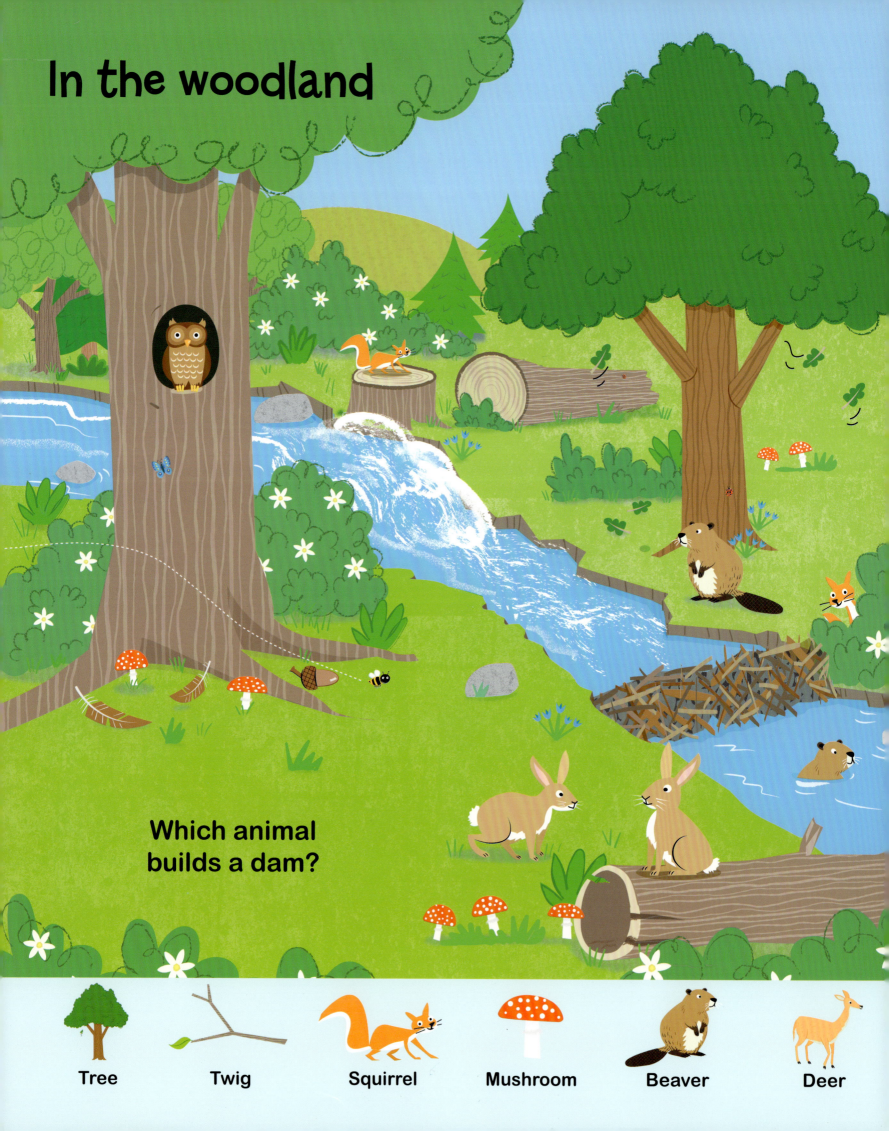

Which animal builds a dam?

| Tree | Twig | Squirrel | Mushroom | Beaver | Deer |

What noise do
bees make?

There are 8 bees, can
you find them all?

Wolf

Rabbit

Bee

Beehive

Can you spot
the acorn?

In the rainforest

What animal is drinking from the river?

Fern Lizard Sloth Monkey Tapir Banana

What noise do monkeys make?

Flowers

Parrot

Vine

Jaguar

Can you spot the butterfly?

In the ocean

Can you spot all 5 starfish?

Dolphin **Shark** **Fin** **Coral** **Turtle** **Ray**

Which animal has 8 tentacles?

Which fish above is facing the wrong way?

Seaweed

Starfish

Octopus

Shell

Can you spot the crab?

In the grassland

How many
elephants are there?

Wildebeest

Hippopotamus

Elephant

Rhino

Zebra

Giraffe

What path leads the baby ostrich to its family?

What noise does a lion make?

Can you spot the lion?

Vulture

Gazelle

Ostrich

Cheetah

In the mountains

Bear

Fish

Yak

Moose

Mountain goat

Snow leopard

How many stars are in the sky?

Is snow hot or cold?

Eagle

Rock

Moon

Stars

Can you spot the pinecone?

In the pond

Can you spot the differences between the dragonflies?

Frog

Reeds

Dragonfly

Duck

Duckling

Lily pad

Can you jump
like a frog?

How many lily pads
can you see?

Rain

Cloud

Log

Snail

Can you
spot the newt?

In the polar region

How many seals
can you see?

Polar bear   Bear cub   Seal   Penguin   Fox   Walrus

Which penguin has an egg?

Which path leads the bear cub back to the adult polar bear?

Can you spot the puffin?

Iceberg   Orca   Reindeer   Narwhal

In the treetops

Which egg is the odd one out?

Branch

Apple

Nest

Wing

Egg

Sparrow

What noise does an owl make?

Caterpillar

Ivy

Owl

Leaf

Can you spot the feather?

In the meadow

What is in the sky?

Which animal has 8 legs?

Spider

Worm

Rainbow

Grass

Corn

Seeds

How many ants
are there?

Grasshopper

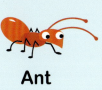
Ant

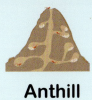
Anthill

Slug

Can you spot
the mouse?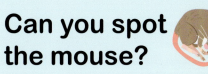

In the swamp

Which animal has sharp teeth?

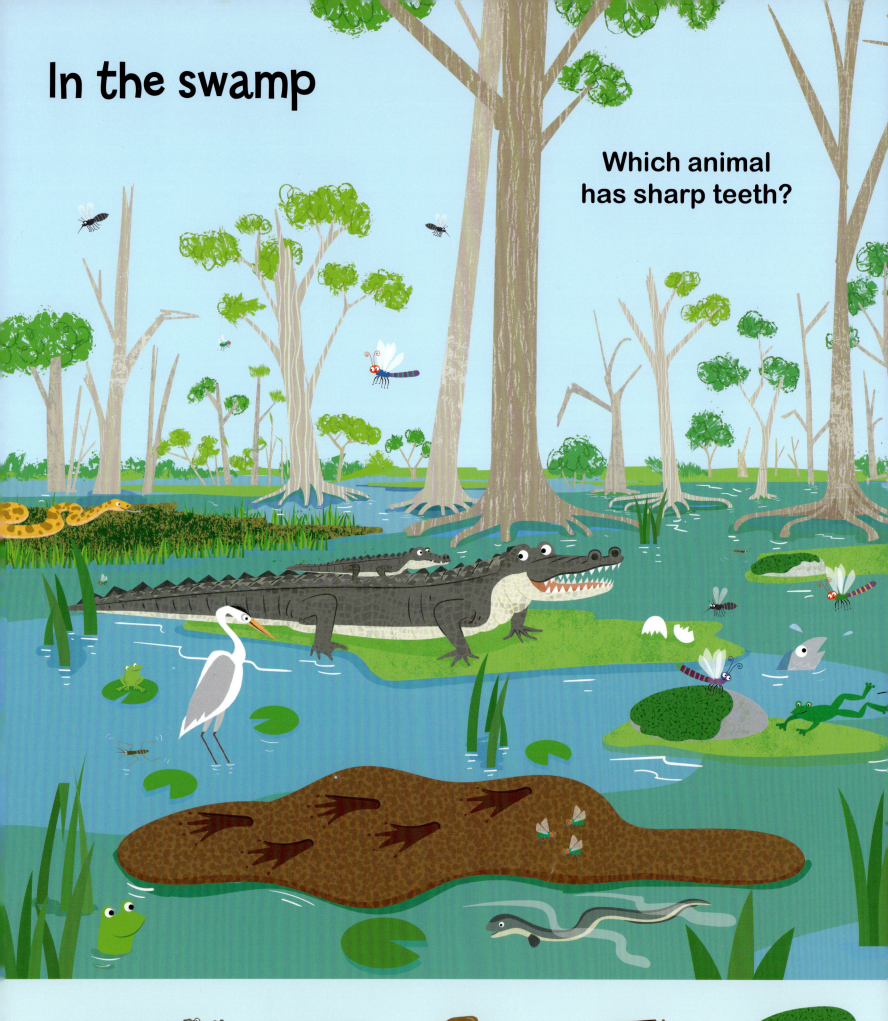

Alligator

Hatchling
(baby alligator)

Mud

Footprint

Moss